Beats of Love

BEATS OF LOVE

A SPACE OPERA ROMANCE NOVELLA

JACQUELINE WESTWOODS

HELIOPOLIS PRESS

HONG KONG

This is a work of fiction.

Names, characters, places, and incidents either are products of the author's imagination or are used fictitiously.

Any similarity to actual events or locales or persons, living or dead, is entirely coincidental.

BEATS OF LOVE

Copyright © 2024 by Jacqueline Westwoods

All rights reserved.

No part of this publication may be reproduced, distributed, or transmitted in any form or by any means, including photocopying, recording, or other electronic or mechanical methods, without the prior written permission of the publisher, except in the case of brief quotations embodied in critical reviews and certain other noncommercial uses permitted by copyright law.

Published by
HELIOPOLIS PRESS

Unit B, 12F, 28 Yee Wo Street
Causeway Bay, Hong Kong

www.heliopolis.press

Heliopolis Press® is a registered trademark of
Heliopolis Creative and Culture Limited

www.heliopolis-cc.com

The Hong Kong Public Library has cataloged the
<u>hardcover</u> edition as follows:

Name: Westwoods, Jacqueline. Author.
Title: Beats of Love / Jacqueline Westwoods.
Description: First edition. | Hong Kong: Heliopolis Press, 2024.
Identifiers: ISBN 978-988-70531-1-8 (ebook)
Subjects: Science Fiction | Romance
Classification: F | Fiction

ISBN 978-988-70531-2-5 (Hardcover)

Our books may be purchased in bulk for promotional, educational, or business use. Please contact your local bookseller or the Heliopolis Press Sales Department by email at sale@heliopolis.press

First Edition: August, 2024
First Hardcover Edition: August, 2024

Printed in Hong Kong

All for Alexandre Dumas, père.

TABLE OF CONTENTS

Chapter 1 - A Deep Crash 1

Chapter 2 - The Sunset 26

Chapter 3 - The Gravity 52

CHAPTER 1

A Deep Crash

In the thin air of the imperial capital, Zafirah, a small combat airship wounded like a young bird, teetered precariously.

This "Swift" hailed from the Velastrion star system, a crowning technological achievement of the Miranor family.

Yet, in Zafirah, it found itself redundant—devoid of the robust atmospheres and wind power, with few terrestrial creatures from old Earth able to survive on the surface.

Zafirah, the sole habitable exoplanet of Estelar Lothringen, was, relatively speaking, "habitable"—a veritable paradise compared to other planets in this star system.

In some respects, it truly was "paradise"—for it served as the capital of the human empire that governed two-thirds of the known galaxy.

Despite the nobility's disdain for the drab

subterranean palaces and the terrifying legends of mass purges, none could resist coveting the entire Lothringen star system's mineral riches and the imperial armoury.

Unknown to many, the former imperial rulers, the Eldaric family, had left behind a perilous legacy.

Yet all were aware that, with the Drakov family's ascension, Gavin I had become the most powerful and threatening man in the galaxy.

However, for Valeria piloting the "Swift", the greatest threat remained of Zafirah's aberrant gravitational pull.

"Damn, this gravitational field..."

Valeria cursed, in a manner unbefitting of a noblewoman, bemoaning the dire straits.

The engine was half-dead, and the other half on the brink of failure.

The chaotic gravitational field was the major culprit, but Valeria knew her own recklessness was the true executioner of the "Swift".

As the jewel in the crown of the Miranor family, lady Valeria possessed exquisite combat airship piloting skills, much like her illustrious mother, Markgräfin Evelina.

These skills had been honed day and night at their home planet Celisara's natural airfields, composed of floating islands and seas of clouds that resembled a celestial realm.

Valeria was her mother's pride, yet she lacked confidence.

At her age, the Markgräfin Evelina had already conquered myriad starry skies, glowing as a star of the empire.

This fledgling, never having ventured beyond her homeworld, longed to spread her wings on another planet.

Even in a non-combative setting, Valeria sought to prove herself in an uncharted domain.

Alas, she had chosen poorly.

This was Zafirah, the most impregnable fortress in the galaxy, painstakingly constructed by emperors over thousands of years—the planet itself a colossal gravitational emitter.

Although Valeria had secured the permits before departing, the imperial construction would not cease for her dreams of flight; at best, they would not regard her "Swift" as an enemy to be shot down.

These works lay hidden beneath Zafirah's surface, entwined with the opulent subterranean palaces— just as intertwined as the empire's power itself.

Unfamiliar with the workings of the gravitational mechanisms, Valeria often circled the same spot, finally realising the complexity of the situation after burning out a primary engine.

She had long heard that the empire's gravitational wave weapons could strike star systems from afar, and everyone was oblivious to how many pitiable mining planets had been hollowed out in the cosmos by the emperors as a deterrent network of firepower, set up at the doorsteps of other families' territories.

Zafirah's own mineral resources had been depleted long ago, but the energy reserves on the sixteen super-heavy planets of Lothringen seemed inexhaustible, at least for thousands of years.

This imperial capital planet also boasted three moons, one natural and two artificial, their presence further complicating the already elusive gravitational field of the capital.

No one could destroy these pinnacles of human ingenuity — unless from within.

Valeria did not wish to bring shame upon her mother, thus hesitating to send out a distress signal.

She did not want to be seen falling, though she could guess that the imperial defence forces might watch her blunder from their monitors, laughing uproariously: Look at that country bumpkin from the imperial fringes, attempting to conquer the skies under the great Emperor's protection!

However, she still prevented this embarrassment from being broadcast.

The Swift's superb capabilities had been fine-tuned for potential malfunctions, and it still subtly maintained its balance under Valeria's control, its visual and navigational trajectory betraying no hint of any problem.

After all, on her home planet Celisara, a fall meant plunging into a nitrogen abyss, becoming a frozen sentinel for the Eternal Night Empress.

Hence, their artificial fliers were ingeniously designed to maintain balance even after a total loss of power.

"Just need to make an emergency landing in an uninhabited area, then contact Josephine afterward —"

Valeria rapidly operated the controls as she had been trained, while plotting her next move.

Though Zafirah was almost an artificial planet, its surface still kept its original appearance—rock and debris interspersed with rare water sources, and sparse vegetation scattered insufficiently to form a continuous cover.

The topography was rugged with mountains and lacked any signs of weathering, as it had been for perhaps hundreds of millions of years.

Valeria sought a relatively flat area for an emergency landing, but neither the sensors nor her eyes could find a suitable spot.

"Water? Where is there water?"

She frantically searched the various waveforms displayed on the scanner for a landing site.

After losing the primary engine, the controls for a vertical landing were no longer reliable.

Coupled with the complex gravitational field, Valeria despaired as her trusty spacecraft silently moaned in distress.

"Empress, I swear I'll never forget to pray to you before setting off again!"

Valeria helplessly tried to recall the verses of the 'Eternal Night Scriptures' she usually skimmed, finding nothing useful, only able to mock herself.

Just then, a buzzing sound plunged her heart into the abyss—probably a change in the gravitational field had knocked out the backup engine, too.

Now only two auxiliary engines were working, but they did not sustain the ship's flight, only just keep it gliding.

In that moment, Valeria desperately realised a head lay in a bottomless chasm.

The tiny "Swift" plummeted into the abyss.

Just as Valeria's vision darkened, and she was about to crash into the mountainside because of the descent, her pilot instincts kicked in, causing her to spin the aircraft around.

After the screech of twisting metal and several collisions, Valeria found, somewhat miraculously, that although the aircraft had completely lost power, it still hovered on the brink of operational death.

Now she was sideways, plunging into a vast crevice.

The dark fissure swallowed the tiny bird like the gaping maw of an Ouroboros.

Relying solely on the chaotic images from her sensors, Valeria continued to maintain control, instinctively.

Though she was feeling dizzy.

The dashboard lit up with intermingling red and yellow lines, and alarms blared incessantly.

After enduring this for what seemed like an eternity, suddenly, a flash of blue zipped past.

That reflective waveform... was it water?

Valeria was both surprised and puzzled.

"Yes! The thin atmosphere doesn't allow most surface water to last long—this is a river valley! An underground river valley!"

She murmured to herself, buoying her spirits.

"Come on, Valeria!"

Although landing in water in the wrong posture could still cause significant damage, Valeria had no other choice; she had to try.

She took a deep breath and then put on her emergency protective mask.

Her maid and personal physician, Sylvia from the Akaza star system, had specifically warned her before departure—Zafirah's atmosphere was thin, and although it had a high oxygen content, for most humans, the surface was a deadly zone where a breathing mask was always necessary.

Otherwise, why would the emperors choose to live in the sunlight-deprived underground?

Her right hand gripped the control stick tightly. And with her left hand, she disengaged the emergency brake needed for manual control.

Her protective suit activated, and the warnings on the dashboard ceased, switching to manual operation.

"Search for the most suitable area for emergency landing," she commanded.

The echo system brought good news; there indeed was a calm body of water ahead—although unknown what lay beneath it—and it existed in a cavernous underground space, vast as a Solutrean cave.

Valeria began the emergency landing.

She felt as though her body was no longer her own, mechanically executing all the actions.

Even her breathing seemed controlled, creating immense internal pressure...

But in that moment, just that instant, the vibrations and impacts from the craft finally snapped Valeria back to reality.

She was mere millimetres from the water's surface, but she held on!

The 'Swift,' after its sharp descent, intermittently flapped its wings—its wings rhythmically vibrating under manual pilot control, occasionally skimming the water's surface.

Because of limited space, Valeria let the craft adopt a spiralling descent to increase gliding distance.

After rotating for a while, it was half-grounded to a halt.

"Did I make it?!"

At first, relief washed over her, but soon deeper worries set in—the darkness enveloped everything.

With the faint light from her craft and the noise it made, she felt like a beacon in the night, an obvious target.

For self-defence, Valeria retrieved a small battle-axe from the semi-jammed cockpit, a weapon of choice in Celisara where the atmospheric conditions favoured melee combat: light-based weapons refracted unpredictably, and the wind blew away physical bullets.

She cautiously slid out of the cockpit, making as little noise as possible to avoid tipping the aircraft into the water.

On her home planet, with its limited land, there were many such water landing sites.

The 'Swift' was designed for flight; it was very light, with a large surface area, and its special design allowed it to float perfectly on water.

Valeria took cover behind a damaged panel on the outside of the cockpit, her feet on the wing and her back against the hull, gripping the battle-axe tightly to her chest.

Her eyes were wide open in the pitch darkness.

She missed nothing.

In this unfamiliar and frightening darkness, Valeria was acting entirely on instinct.

Suddenly, a light flickered nearby, like a fairy's lantern.

No, it couldn't be fire—Zafirah's atmosphere couldn't support such a light source—it must be something else.

The alien princess strained to see what the faint light source was—then she saw a humanoid figure, presumably also human, carrying a transparent container filled with a flickering pale blue light.

Not just one person, but suddenly, it seemed as if the stars themselves had lit up, with weak, twinkling lights surrounding the water.

She could now see the environment she was in: a huge cavern, with footing all around, filled with people wearing ragged cloaks and breathing masks.

A figure who seemed to be the leader stepped forward.

"Who are you?" the person demanded sharply, the voice carrying anger and a hint of fear.

It was a woman's voice, speaking the imperial common tongue precisely, with no accent, albeit less refined than the aristocracy.

But Valeria understood her perfectly—only the voice was very weak.

"I am lost, and my flyer is broken," she called out, with her voice muffled by the uncomfortable mask.

But her voice did not carry.

And after shouting for a while, she realised that

the dense atmosphere here probably wouldn't support the transmission of her weak voice over any distance.

Valeria crawled back into the cockpit and used the communicator's amplifier to repeat, "I mean no harm. My ship has failed. And I had to make an emergency landing here!"

"Drop your weapon. We are from the 'Viper Squad.'"

Poor Valeria didn't understand what that title meant.

Her knowledge of the imperial capital was still limited to textbooks—though the practical lesson she'd just endured had taught her a harsh lesson and caused her much distress.

"I will comply. I mean no harm," she repeated.

As she spoke, she attempted to throw the axe into the water to show her sincerity.

"Stop—"

She froze.

"Do not throw foreign contaminants into the Sacred Lake!" another agitated man increased the amplifier's volume, causing a screech that made everyone wearing electronic communication devices wince.

So the lake water was sacred to them!

The young lady withdrew her weapon.

Following their instructions, Valeria placed the battle-axe back in the cockpit and kept her hands raised as she crouched on the wing.

Several people were dispatched from the other side,

bringing with them what looked like a shuttle-shaped wooden board.

They let it float on the water surface—then the woman who spoke the standard common tongue stepped onto it, being gently pushed towards Valeria.

The woman seemed to have outstanding balance, controlling the wooden board with her feet, directing it, and coming to a steady stop in front of Valeria.

"Get on. I'll push you across. Don't move around, or you'll fall into hell," she warned Valeria.

"Can this carry the weight of two people?"

Valeria cautiously stood up, worried about the fragility of this thin slab compared to her craft.

"Don't worry, I'll adjust my position to the other end to balance it," the woman said, with her voice carrying a hint of peculiarity.

She deliberately lowered her voice, speaking only to Valeria, "I don't want to fall in either, and don't fantasise about swimming away. They call it the 'Sacred Lake.' But really, it's just wastewater from imperial constructions, with radioactive materials and other types of mineral contaminants under the lake."

The woman sized up Valeria and continued, "Your flight suit is good, it's sealed—that saved you from the contamination of the lake water. I'll take that suit. Agree to give it to me, and I'll let you fend for yourself on the surface."

Valeria didn't know what to contest at that moment: staying alive was enough.

She asked apprehensively.

"The respirator is integrated with the suit."

"We can give you a used one, but I don't know how much reserve it has left. Tsk, you alien, don't separate your respirators from your clothing? Seems I can't sell it then. But I quite like this suit. I'll keep it in exchange for your life."

"Should I say 'Thank you, ma'am'?"

Valeria muttered softly and carefully followed the woman into the floating wood.

The woman slowly backed away while exclaiming, "Not bad for balance, alien girl. Where did you serve? Those Ironmen don't have your skills. Nor do they have your little toy."

"Ironmen" seemed to refer to the imperial guard, as they had to wear full-body exoskeletons to move conveniently on Zafirah's surface.

"It's not a toy! It's a flyer! And I'm not even a soldier yet!"

Valeria felt deflated: her mother still did not acknowledge that she could handle combat alone and had not allowed her to join the combat troops.

"You're not a soldier?"

The woman looked very puzzled. But amidst the urging from the surrounding others, she fired something hidden in her cloak that lodged into the surrounding rock walls.

It was a steel wire, allowing the two of them to be pulled back to the shore on a pulley system, away from the dangerous lake waters.

This was how they normally moved across the water. Valeria thought.

Though her life was still in the hands of others, her curiosity now overcame her fear.

Valeria looked around, taking in everything under the faint glimmering lights reflected around her.

She noticed people entering the cave at the other end of the lake, causing a commotion. But she was too far away to see or hear clearly.

As they neared the shore, the woman signalled for Valeria to move towards the middle of the board.

And then, with the help of two young boys, they were successfully pulled ashore.

Valeria breathed a sigh of relief.

The solid ground under her feet finally gave her a moment of peace after the prolonged tension.

But at that moment, fear gripped her again as she remembered her recent ordeal, and the suffocating, oppressive feelings resurfaced.

"Hey, give me your suit," demanded the woman.

"The big sister wants her suit, what do we get?" the two boys—more accurately, the little imps—asked discontentedly.

"You get that metal clunker if you can bring it over."

"No, that is—"

"Geoffrey's back!"

Before Valeria could finish her protest, several adolescents nearby cheered.

Was he their leader?

Valeria noticed the woman was becoming anxious —she repeated, "Quick, give me your suit," and handed her a tattered respirator.

The mask was dirty and repulsive, and Valeria, already reluctant to change in front of everyone, hesitated even more.

But to save her own life, she felt she should comply with the demand, as she lacked the confidence to fight off so many people and escape the unfamiliar canyon alone.

Just as she was about to hold her breath and remove her own mask, a clear voice came through.

"You'll die."

It was like a crisp breeze whispering in her ear.

Valeria felt a shiver. She didn't even recognise herself. And she just dumbly complied.

Confused, she saw the man they called Geoffrey approach—apparently; he was the source of the voice.

A medium-built young man, only slightly taller than Valeria, walked towards her.

Beneath his ragged cloak, she could see a pair of glossy, metallic boots—she couldn't see his face clearly, as his mask was in stealth mode.

Was he an imperial soldier?!

What was happening?

Valeria was filled with doubts.

He was an "Ironman," supposedly an ally; but he seemed to be well integrated with this group...

His heavy iron boots were sleekly designed, and the entire exoskeleton's structure was so meticulously and solemnly crafted—his well-trained, steady steps made his footfalls seem like the drumbeats of a war god, resonant and imbued with a sacred aura.

Ironman Geoffrey approached the woman, seemingly angry.

"Do you want her to die here?"

"Tch... Whether she willingly dies here or gets played to death by those bastards outside, I'm making it look nicer. If she takes off that mask, she'll be a walking poison zombie within five minutes," the woman argued heatedly.

"You could have waited for me to come back," Geoffrey said somewhat helplessly, patting her shoulder.

The woman was unappreciative, shrugging him off and turning to leave.

Her voice floated back faintly, "Those 'Celestials' and the Iron Guard are all the same. I have done nothing wrong."

Their conversation made Valeria suddenly realise what she had just been through, and fear surged, overwhelming her last bit of rationality.

She collapsed weakly to the ground, eyeing Geoffrey warily, and asked, "Did you steal that Iron Guard uniform?"

Geoffrey shook his head.

"No, this is my gear. I'm still an imperial soldier," he said, with his voice lacking confidence.

Valeria, still harbouring doubts, asked, "So, you came to rescue me?"

She had already been deceived once and was wary of being gullible again, feeling a strong resistance.

Her mind buzzed, unsure whether to trust him...

"Yes," Geoffrey answered, "I saw your flight trajectory was unusual from the monitoring station. And since this area is their sanctuary, I was worried your crash landing in Viper territory could cause political issues."

Noticing her distrust stemming from her recent deception, he added, "I sympathise with these people, so I've been secretly supplying them with goods. You can trust me, and my actions are authorised; I'm not a rebel."

"So... the guard knows?"

Valeria's emotions surged, realising he rescued her.

She could survive! She wouldn't die from a saving face in the imperial sewers!

She suddenly stood up, but in the moment of cerebral insufficiency, she realised this might mean her actions would soon become known to her mother and peers, and to the imperial nobility—not just facing a scolding from her mother and punishment at home anymore, but now she might embarrass her mother and cause political problems!

These intense emotions made Valeria lose direction again, and she desperately tried to control herself.

"I have told no one else," he quickly added.

"Really?"

"Only I noticed your trajectory was off. And even if your machine hadn't malfunctioned, I was worried they might mistreat a princess from another planet," Geoffrey further explained.

This explanation somewhat convinced Valeria, but she retorted discontentedly.

"I'm not some princess! I..."

"You are Markgräfin Evelina's daughter. So, to these locals, who are full of hostility towards the nobility: you are the evil alien princess—"

"—That has nothing to do with my mother!"

She was angry because people on her planet also disliked imperial affairs. She felt helpless because what Geoffrey said was true.

His words were direct, cold, and painful, but Valeria could sense the complex emotions beneath his icy metallic mask.

She tried to step forward but tripped over an unseen dip in the dark terrain, losing her balance.

Valeria fell forward, tumbling right into Geoffrey's arms.

It was a somewhat hard and uncomfortable embrace, but it supported her steadily.

His arms gently shielded her to prevent her from falling and breaking her mask, becoming a toxic zombie.

"Sorry..." she murmured, feeling a bit embarrassed as she pushed herself away, still unsteady on her feet.

He smiled wryly.

"It seems you haven't fully recovered. You did well on the floating wood just now."

"You saw it?"

"Yes, I saw everything. I could tell you were well-trained; no wonder you're..."

Geoffrey seemed to suddenly realise the crux of the issue and swallowed the rest of his sentence.

The two stood in silence for several seconds, both feeling awkward about the topic.

Finally, Geoffrey extended his hand.

"Have you recovered now? If not, hold on to my hand."

Valeria complied, as she was still feeling unsteady and lacked night vision equipment to see the terrain clearly.

So, the two of them, under the watchful eyes of many, moved towards the cave exit.

Along the narrow lakeshore, Geoffrey led the anxious Valeria slowly forward.

Her eyes adjusted to the environment, and as more people gathered with those strange lamps, everything around her slowly became clear from the darkness.

The enormous underground lake was pitch black and unfathomable, its surface reflecting the faint light from the shore, like a silver ringed crown.

Valeria's poor aircraft floated in the middle of the lake, shining brightly, like an idol for worship.

The surrounding people were dressed in tattered cloth and wore those old breathing masks, their bodies wrapped up tightly.

Valeria could sense a lot of hostility and curiosity from their postures.

Considering her recent ordeal, she should have been scared—but somehow, Geoffrey's arm reassured her.

You're too naïve, Valeria! He and that woman must be acting in concert to further deceive you and harm your mother...

This contradictory mindset gradually plunged her back into fear.

So, just as they were about to exit the cave, Valeria let go of Geoffrey's arm, swiftly sidestepped, and drew a small knife from her sleeve.

The black Ironman remained motionless, seemingly unsurprised by her reaction.

"Of course, it would be foolish to trust so easily," Geoffrey said, spreading his hands.

"What do you really want?" Valeria asked, trembling.

"Let me put it another way... I am a lower-level soldier secretly sympathetic to these people, part of the Defence Department. I manipulated the gravity defence net to trap you and lead you here. I won't harm you because I want to gain my superiors' trust by rescuing you. Your safety is more beneficial to me... Does that explanation make sense?"

This explanation sounded more plausible, making Valeria somewhat convinced.

She continued to ask, "Aren't you afraid your superiors will find out you tampered with the defence net? Or that I'll expose you once I'm rescued?"

Geoffrey chuckled lightly, "Because the Imperial Guard are all incredibly arrogant, and you are an 'alien princess,' they won't fully believe you. They might even suspect you and your mother of colluding with the rebels. As for me, I would be seen as a mere pawn bought off by you... That scenario isn't what you want, is it?"

His words were clear and incisive: Valeria's family would face a political crisis because of her impulsive bravery, while he, a soldier prepared to die, would at most lose his life.

Seeing that Valeria's combat stance had relaxed a bit, Geoffrey further explained, "But you saw it, too. Those people are fierce but still no match for the regular army. Plus, there are many old and weak among them; I don't want to bring war here..."

Valeria nodded.

She had seen for herself that those half-grown children wouldn't stand a chance against her, and the warriors by the lake, fighting in such a narrow and dangerous area, would have some reservations.

If she could take down the female scammer from earlier, she would have a good chance of escaping.

If she had seen everything clearly, she might have judged differently regarding their combat capabilities. She might have taken the risk of fighting her way out once off the lake.

But she had no actual combat experience and had killed no one, so she backed down.

Her mother was right: she wasn't qualified to be a soldier yet, nor was she ready to inherit everything from her mother.

Valeria sheathed her knife.

"May I ask for a favour?"

For the first time, she looked directly at the mysterious young man named Geoffrey.

"Go ahead."

"I can help you keep these things secret, but I hope you can help me retrieve my craft—if that's not possible, then sink it into that wastewater..."

"Sinking it is too dangerous... Aside from the cave dwellers' faith issues, do you know why the Imperial City developed non-explosive defence devices? They were afraid any noise would cause the surface to collapse, destroying underground structures,"

Geoffrey replied earnestly.

"As for retrieving it, if we can fix the engine, it might be possible. Unfortunately, I'm a soldier, not a mechanic, and I can't help you find outsiders..."

Hearing this good news, Valeria's mood finally brightened.

"That's great! I have a mechanic I absolutely trust —"

"But I might not trust them, and they might not trust me either," Geoffrey's reply poured cold water on her excitement.

Valeria's heart sank.

She leaned weakly against the dim tunnel wall, muttering to herself in a voice only she could hear, "If Mother were here, what would she do..."

"What's wrong? Are you feeling unwell? Is there a breach in your suit?"

Geoffrey, not understanding the situation, suddenly seemed nervous.

He tried to reach out to support Valeria, but she batted his hand away.

"You—"

"Really, are you alright?"

"I'm fine. None of your business. Besides, wouldn't it be better for you if I died here? At least you wouldn't have to worry about me revealing this place," Valeria replied irritably.

Her emotions seemed to be affected by something, suddenly becoming agitated.

Facing this young gentleman, her heart was pounding, and she felt a strange resistance to his excessive concern.

Geoffrey was stunned. Something seemed to stir within him as well.

Valeria found this situation made her feel breathless—not because of the oxygen concentration, but because Geoffrey's presence gave her an unprecedented sense of oppression, one she couldn't describe.

As the two were locked in this standoff, another set of footsteps approached.

"She's right. It would be better if she died here. At least she has the self-awareness," a woman's voice slowly emerged from the darkness.

Both turned towards the voice to see the female scammer from earlier, who seemed to have been watching the drama unfold, now leaning casually against the cave wall ahead.

The scammer continued, "My dear Geoffrey, you are nothing but a wandering soul in the underground void—you don't know what you are, or what you want. That's why you're so conflicted. Your hesitation between kindness and cruelty will only harm everyone."

Valeria didn't understand why she suddenly came out spouting such incomprehensible philosophy, but she sensed that Geoffrey's emotions were becoming more intense because of the woman's words.

Strange, why could she feel his thoughts? And why did she somewhat understand what the woman was saying?

Strange.

Geoffrey's armour trembled at a frequency

imperceptible to humans.

"Get back! She's going to attack you!"

Geoffrey's sudden warning startled Valeria, causing her to take a step back instinctively.

She kept her eyes fixed on the enemy, but the woman seemed oblivious to their commotion.

"Geoffrey, you're still too weak. Let me decide for you," the woman said.

Suddenly, she flicked a sleeve arrow from her wrist, aiming straight at Valeria, who was still processing the conversation's implications.

Valeria couldn't dodge in time, as the wall behind her restricted her movements. She could only try to evade to the side...

A loud "clang" echoed.

Geoffrey's iron armour deflected the sleeve arrow, producing a metallic sound.

"Hmph, it seems you've already made your choice..." the woman sneered.

Geoffrey's emotions were still in turmoil, but he was no longer confused.

He scooped Valeria up around the waist, activated the jets on his back, and launched them away.

"Mr Geoffrey?!"

Valeria exclaimed, feeling a mix of confusion, delight, and anxiety.

Geoffrey, focused on controlling the flight device, didn't respond immediately.

The rapid low-altitude flight didn't frighten Valeria.

She even felt a bit exhilarated.

To avoid falling, she clung tightly to Geoffrey until

they landed in the shadow of a rock formation on the surface.

"That was insane! Oh my goodness! What are you trying to do?!"

Valeria cried out, breaking free from Geoffrey as soon as the immediate crisis was over.

"I... I just..."

Geoffrey, exhausted, collapsed to the ground.

"I just wanted to save you. I don't want to see anyone get killed..."

He pounded the ground with his fist and shook his head vehemently.

"She was right; my hesitation will harm everyone."

"That woman... She first saved me, then deceived me, and finally tried to kill me?"

Geoffrey gave a bitter smile.

"No, an Archon possessed her."

"Archons?" Valeria was shocked.

Her mother had taught her that Archons were one of the most dangerous species in the universe: elusive, without physical form, capable of controlling human minds, and had once infiltrated human society by using human cloning technology, creating a special race known as the Archontes.

The Empire had always opposed the existence of archontes, legislating against human cloning and strictly controlling related technologies to prevent Archons from exploiting them.

Encountering an Archon in the heart of the Empire's power, the capital, was both eerie and dangerous.

"At least, I believe so..." Geoffrey replied solemnly.

"That wasn't the 'Viper' squad leader Nina I know. And I've encountered that Archon before; his tone..."

Valeria sensed something was amiss.

"So how did you know she was going to attack me?" she asked, puzzled.

"Did you realise an Archon possessed her?"

Geoffrey paused, then slowly stood up. He shook his head lightly and said, "I don't remember warning you..."

An indescribable fear welled up in Valeria's heart.

She felt as if some mental force had controlled her back in the underground cave... right at the moment before she fell.

Valeria's heart sank to the bottom.

CHAPTER 2

The Sunset

The terminator line gradually approached the bare rock wall where the two stood.

The thin atmosphere caused the sunset to fall at an astonishing speed—this was how darkness descended upon the Imperial Capital.

"Were you possessed, too? Were we almost taken over by those creatures?"

Valeria looked at Geoffrey, whose figure was gradually being swallowed by the shadow of the rocks.

"That's unlikely."

Geoffrey seemed to regain his composure.

"The protective suits of the Imperial Army are specially designed to resist their mental invasion."

"What about me?!"

Valeria couldn't believe it.

Geoffrey waved his hand, making a stopping gesture, signalling her not to overthink.

"Didn't they teach you on Celisara how to identify and defend against them? It's quite simple. Archons don't have childhoods; they are high-dimensional spiritual beings. Therefore, whether they create containers like archontes or possess other intelligent beings, they can't fabricate memories of a childhood. Also, they cannot easily invade the brain of an already conscious being; otherwise, they wouldn't need to create clone containers specifically. When they invade, you will distinctly feel it—according to some survivors, it feels like another personality is fighting for control of your mind; your senses will also enter their dimension, witnessing heights that human consciousness can't reach. This mutual erosion is uncontrollable, and they don't want us 'lower species' to know too much about their side of things."

Valeria thought back carefully, feeling somewhat relieved that she hadn't been fully invaded.

"Maybe it tried to invade me, which could explain my crash... But I feel normal now, with none of those special sensory experiences you mentioned."

"Good. I must get you back quickly. Besides, it's already dark. Staying on the surface any longer, your life-support system won't hold up for much longer."

With that, Geoffrey made a "please, this way" gesture, signalling for Valeria to follow him down the rocky cliff.

Valeria couldn't help but laugh.

"Are you serious?"

"Oh... my apologies."

He seemed to have forgotten that Valeria, as an alien visitor, didn't have the equipment to move easily over rugged terrain.

Geoffrey retracted his hand and extended it towards Valeria.

"If you don't mind..."

Valeria thought it wasn't a big deal initially, but his serious reminder made it somewhat awkward.

However, she didn't hesitate and extended her hand to Geoffrey to support her.

Geoffrey gently lifted her up, in stark contrast to his earlier roughness.

Although he was still clad in that cold black armour, Valeria felt as if the icy exterior had melted slightly, making her feel warm.

The low-altitude flight continued for a while.

"Will you... will you report that woman? Because an Archon possessed her?"

Valeria's intuition told her that his relationship with the woman was unusual, so she curiously asked.

"If you're worried that I will betray Nina, I won't. She is my foster sister. We grew up together in an orphanage."

"An orphanage? In such a barren place... there's an orphanage?"

"It's in the civilian quarters—we'll pass by there when we go through the underground city. Nina and I, like you, are not originally from the caves. Later, I joined the army to support my livings, but she chose a different path."

"Won't the Archon take over her body completely? Or other Troglodytes' bodies?"

"That one should be what the Troglodytes call 'The Phantom.' It's said to have existed for thousands of years, guiding them on how to survive. When I said I might have seen it, it was because Nina told me—at some gathering, she pointed out a priest instructing the followers and said, 'Look, that's The Phantom.' When I looked at him, he suddenly made eye contact with me—I wasn't wearing a protective suit and I felt something touching my mind. But in the end, it did nothing. Maybe it wasn't in that person or perhaps it wasn't interested in invading me."

"So, it's their god?"

"Some Troglodytes worship it, while others fear it. Sometimes it possesses its followers to deliver 'divine messages' and sometimes it kills some Troglodytes—for reasons unknown to people."

"The Empire turns a blind eye to this?" Valeria was surprised, as her history lessons about the Archons never mentioned such an entity.

"Yes, and what's even stranger is that 'The Phantom' seems to have a sort of tacit understanding: it never invades the underground cities of civilians, let alone the underground fortresses where the nobility live. Its existence must be a scandal for the rulers..."

"Indeed."

This implied some sort of failure, error, and vulnerability.

Valeria suddenly thought about her own 'scandal'—if her unfortunate crash was made public, it would undoubtedly cause a huge stir and a significant political crisis.

But fortunately, she now believed that the suspicious and terrifying happenings in the Troglodyte cave wouldn't spread—at least not through the person who saved her—and at most, she would only lose her aircraft.

The thought still pained her.

For Valeria, it wasn't just her coming-of-age gift. It was also her mother's recognition of her...

If she were to be punished, she would prefer only her mother to know. She thought silently, wanting to see her mother as soon as possible.

The Ironman's flight device soon brought her to a place that looked like a valley.

"Is this the entrance to the underground city?"

"Yes, it's a very hidden one. Most residents are unaware of it. I discovered it by chance during a surface patrol."

Geoffrey led her through a place that seemed completely seamless—the crack was at such an angle that it was impossible to see its depth from any distance!

Inside the crevice was a metal wall, with a piece of metal slightly lifted.

"Ordinary people wouldn't be able to move it, but our exoskeleton suits can," Geoffrey explained, then showed the gap to Valeria.

"If you remember your promise..."

Valeria reminded Geoffrey, trying to overcome her fear of the unknown.

Although she felt Geoffrey was hiding many things from her, she sensed his concern for her was genuine.

This feeling was remarkable, as if their souls were connected—through flesh, through artificial armour, through millions of stars.

"Don't worry, the Imperial Army won't know. As for how you explain it to the Margravine, that's your own business."

Valeria's cheeks felt hot. She was glad she was still wearing her protective suit.

The two passed through the narrow crevice and arrived at Civilian Settlement No. 3, an underground city.

This area, close to the surface, comprised older air-raid shelters, abandoned factories, and basic defensive structures.

The entrance to the crevice was inside a warehouse of one such factory.

"Here, you can temporarily stop using your life-support system. The air is breathable," Geoffrey said, manipulating his arm device to open his concealed mask and revealing his previously hidden face.

It was a clean, handsome face with deep brown curly hair plastered to his cheeks with sweat, looking dishevelled.

His long eyelashes and dark eyes were captivating.

His demeanour bore some resemblance to Nina's, with rebellious eyebrows that hinted at defiance, yet there was a delicate beauty to him.

If Valeria hadn't heard his voice, she might have thought he and Nina were sisters.

Valeria checked the oxygen levels and air pressure, confirming that there were no issues. She finally opened her stifling mask as well.

She shook her head, suddenly feeling a sharp

smell, and coughed a few times.

It made her seem ridiculous—though, to be fair, while there were no toxic substances.

The micro-dust from the old factories made her nose itch, causing her to embarrass herself in front of him.

"You should put the mask back on until we reach the residential area," Geoffrey suggested resignedly.

Valeria grudgingly closed her mask again.

She noticed a hint of amusement at the corners of his mouth—clearly, her discomfort had entertained him.

Valeria mentally punched him, but outwardly pretended nothing had happened.

Sensing her reaction, Geoffrey quickly turned away and said, "Let's go. You can walk on your own this time."

So they continued toward the residential area.

According to Geoffrey, Underground City No. 3 was one of the moderately well-off civilian areas, with a smaller population and less active industry.

"The wealthier and more active underground cities are deeper down, as they are newer constructions. This place is mostly abandoned, but the upside is that it's less strictly regulated."

When he mentioned "abandoned," Valeria distinctly felt a hint of sadness.

"To keep your presence hidden, I'll take you to the orphanage to borrow some clothes. Otherwise, your suit is too conspicuous and might draw attention from patrols in other areas. We need to go deeper, all the way to the restricted zone."

"The restricted zone?"

"That's where the palace is located," Geoffrey explained.

"Aren't you a lower-ranked soldier?"

"Ahem." This time, Geoffrey coughed.

"I'll explain that later."

Valeria mumbled to herself: How many secrets do you have?

On the way to the orphanage, she kept staring at Geoffrey's back, speculating: Maybe he's actually a high-ranking officer? Or perhaps a mischievous nobleman? Or maybe he's a prince?

As they walked, Geoffrey shared information about the civilian area with intimate knowledge.

"There used to be indoor farming facilities here. But now food production has moved to the orbital stations. So people here gradually moved to other underground cities."

He pointed out a few shops that had existed once, now sealed by time.

Only someone who had grown up here would know these details—but how did he get permission to access the restricted zone?

No matter how she thought about it, each possibility had its own set of contradictions.

Just as Valeria was lost in thought, they arrived at the orphanage.

It was an old hospital that had been repurposed, but it was well-maintained.

The high walls surrounded it. But once inside, it was a different world altogether.

An elderly man greeted them.

Upon seeing Geoffrey, he immediately agreed to his request without a word.

"That's Mr Stephen. He has worked here for over 30 years. He can't speak, but he's very kind to all of us."

Valeria received the borrowed clothes from the wrinkled, smiling Mr Stephen and walked into the changing room.

On her way, she was bumped by a few giggling children—who stopped to curiously look at her, this stranger, with no fear.

"Geoffrey, is that your bride?" one of the older kids loudly asked a man who was heading into another changing room.

"Don't talk nonsense!" Geoffrey warned sternly. "Or I'll have someone come to get you."

"You won't do that; you even let that bad Nina go! Hee hee!"

The kids ignored Geoffrey's warning, shouting as they ran away.

Valeria's face turned red, then white, with embarrassment.

Fortunately, Geoffrey, busy chasing away the onlookers, didn't notice her reaction.

"You're quite popular with the kids," she remarked, quickly heading to change.

The dress she borrowed was faded and simple, loose-fitting and plain.

The material was something Valeria had never encountered before—she didn't know what it was called—but it felt much rougher than what she was used to wearing, though not uncomfortable.

She thought she looked a bit like a doctor or nurse in it.

Geoffrey had changed into a regular military uniform.

Valeria recognised his insignia, which seemed to show a rank of lieutenant—she had seen the insignia on the uniforms of imperial officials' escorts stationed in the Celisara star system, and those of captains had an additional stripe compared to Geoffrey's.

"Alright, if anyone questions us, let me do the talking. If they refuse to let us through, you can reveal your identity... Just say you wanted to experience the local customs of the Imperial Capital?"

"That excuse might work on your people..." Valeria pondered.

"What, you rarely do that?" Geoffrey seemed surprised.

Valeria couldn't help but mentally punch Geoffrey again—was his brain made of stone?

"We don't have such 'zone restrictions' on Celisara. We go wherever we want!" Valeria retorted.

If there was one thing she was known for, it was venturing into flight zones beyond her skill level—just like today.

She couldn't help pacing a few steps, recalling some of the recent experiences. Then she walked back to the changing room and brought out her decent protective suit.

She remembered how Nina had tricked her into handing over her belongings, which were likely precious here.

"Since I overheard a certain lieutenant mention

his childhood, I wanted to donate to the orphanage. That's my reason for this secret visit—"

Before she finished speaking, she gathered any other valuables she had on her.

She knew these items couldn't significantly improve the lives of the orphans or Troglodytes, but it was better than nothing—though a pilot shouldn't carry personal possessions.

She ended up taking off a pair of small earrings.

"—and this."

She thrust the earrings into Geoffrey's hand.

Geoffrey was taken aback by the gesture, speechless for a moment.

Finally, he laughed, a relieved and genuine laugh.

"Thank you on behalf of the children, Lady Valeria."

"You know my name?"

Valeria was taken aback by the familiarity with which Geoffrey addressed her.

This time, it was Geoffrey who blushed.

"Lady Evelina, she seems to want the Emperor to acknowledge you as her successor—this has been the talk of the Imperial Capital lately. Your name is often mentioned here in the court," he mumbled.

Valeria hadn't expected this reason, but she seized the implications.

"Mother is in her prime; how could she be designating me as her successor already?"

Geoffrey didn't respond, instead looking at Valeria with a deep sympathy.

Suddenly, Valeria understood why her mother

had brought her here—there was nothing more valuable to a noble successor than a reliable marriage contract to secure the family's interests.

The Miranor family, on the empire's frontier, had traditionally passed titles through the female line, maintaining their relative independence by marrying into other families without granting them inheritance rights.

Lady Evelina was an exception.

Her status and wealth were earned through her own prowess, with even the Imperial Marshal admiring her military acumen.

She remained unmarried, and Valeria's father's identity remained a mystery.

Valeria had to admit her mother was unique.

She couldn't imagine how her mother had led their small fleet to repel enemies from the dark fringes of the empire without imperial support.

Once in the past, the entire human race had betrayed their family, but Lady Evelina had held firm.

If Valeria asked herself honestly, she knew she couldn't do the same.

Her mother probably recognised that she would need the firm support of other families in the future, and this visit to the Imperial Capital was for her treasured only child.

Without her incompetent daughter, her mother wouldn't need to bow to those vile people.

Valeria felt a deep bitterness.

"Oh, thank you for telling me," Valeria said, not knowing what else to say.

Their journey back to the restricted zone was

smooth, except at the final checkpoint, where they had to reveal their identities.

It turned out Geoffrey was part of a special unit under the Marshal's command—though his rank wasn't high; he had special permissions to enter and leave the restricted zone with the Marshal.

"I can only escort you this far. I must report back to the Marshal's residence. From here, the palace guards will take you to Lady Evelina's temporary quarters," Geoffrey bid her farewell.

There was something flickering in his eyes.

He seemed to have a lot to say to her.

"Will we meet again?" Valeria asked.

Despite their short time together, she couldn't forget him.

Geoffrey thought for a moment, then took out a metal engraved plaque from his pocket.

It bore the emblem of the orphanage, along with his name and number.

"If you ever need help... the Troglodytes and the people at the orphanage recognise this plaque. They will assist you."

"Thank you... So, is this goodbye forever?"

Valeria felt the warmth of the metal, as if it carried Geoffrey's own warmth.

"Goodbye. Fly free, little bird," Geoffrey looked down, unable to meet her eyes.

He knew she might never fly freely again.

Upon receiving news of Valeria's safe arrival, Evelina sent her daughter's peers to meet her.

These young men and women, around Valeria's age, were handpicked by the Markgräfin to assist her daughter.

They harboured immense hostility towards the man who had "abducted" their princess.

Though they restrained themselves out of courtesy, their eyes betrayed their antagonism.

Sensing the tension, Geoffrey tactfully walked away, not waiting for Valeria's last farewell.

She stood there, surrounded by her radiant companions.

Valeria had grown accustomed to such attention since childhood, feeling as though the world revolved around her—until she met Geoffrey.

Her world had changed.

Valeria's heart felt different.

It was as if a living parasite had taken residence, warm yet gnawing at her heart during their separation, causing inexplicable pain.

Her companions criticised the dry, thin air of the Imperial Capital and the ugly underground city or praised her compassion and charity while vying for her favour.

Only one person noticed Valeria's unusual demeanour.

"Are you tired, Valeria?" a weak, somewhat timid voice asked.

Coming to her senses, Valeria saw it was her best friend Josephine and nodded wearily.

"Yes, exhausted."

"Is something wrong, my lady?" Sylvia approached.

As Valeria's personal physician, it was her duty, though she didn't seem as attuned to Valeria's every move as Josephine.

"No, I'm not unwell, just very tired. Sylvia, I want to rest. Josephine will stay with me."

Valeria clung to Josephine.

Together, they returned to Valeria's room, arm in arm.

Valeria finally collapsed, having gone through so much that day.

After washing up, she looked at Josephine, who stayed close by, worried she might faint.

"Can you believe it? That man, he actually —"

She recounted everything that had happened that day, including the crash, the underground valley, the pitiable Troglodytes, the strange Nina, the terrifying Archons, and, of course, Geoffrey, who had been with her throughout.

Valeria confided everything to her close friend; there were no secrets between them.

Yet the weight of it seemed to fall solely on Josephine, as Valeria's mind was filled with thoughts of Geoffrey.

"Get some sleep," Josephine suggested, hearing the fatigue in Valeria's voice.

"But I'm afraid this is just a dream—I'm afraid I'll forget everything when I wake up... Josephine, you wouldn't understand, would you? To meet someone so special, intriguing, and mysterious... someone who you can't stop thinking about. What I've experienced today is more than in the past nineteen years."

"But tomorrow is your debut at the Imperial Capital's social ball. You should rest early tonight," Josephine gently urged.

She had also endured a nerve-wracking day, fearing her friend might not return.

Josephine sighed, gently touching Valeria's warm forehead.

"You're feverish; let me call Sylvia."

"No, I'm not sick!"

Valeria grabbed Josephine's hand.

Valeria knew her friend's concern was not without reason, so she opened up fully.

"I just... I think I might have fallen for someone I met for the first time. It's crazy, but I can't control my heart. Do you think this is the Archons' influence on me?"

"Your experiences today were indeed very complex, and it's hard for me to judge. I'm not an expert on Archons; their impact on our planet is minimal. But I've heard some rumours..."

"Rumours? About Geoffrey?"

Valeria, now excited, pulled her friend closer.

Josephine laughed.

"You've never been this concerned about someone before. Alright, my dear Valeria. Unfortunately, the matter isn't directly about Geoffrey—truthfully, I had never heard of him before. But it relates to his superior."

"His superior... you mean... someone from the Marshal's office?"

Valeria, usually uninterested in Imperial politics, found herself suddenly invested because of Geoffrey.

"Yes, it's about Marshal Thorburn himself. And," Josephine hesitated for a moment before leaning closer to Valeria's ear, "Lady Evelina."

Valeria's eyes widened in shock.

Josephine implored her not to get angry after hearing the next part, as it might be disrespectful to the revered Lady Evelina.

"When Lady Evelina was your age, she received military training in the Imperial Capital, under Marshal Thorburn's guidance. The Marshal was very fond of her, which sparked jealousy and rumours. One such rumour claimed... Marshal Thorburn is your father."

Valeria nearly gasped.

"But Mother often says that Thorburn is the most dangerous figure in the Imperial military to us. She says if Thorburn were to lead an attack, we'd be doomed within three days... She's so formidable, yet fears this man."

"Maybe they know each other very well, which is why she says that..."

Hearing this, Valeria didn't feel upset. Instead, she felt a sense of relief.

"So, Mother didn't come here for my marriage, but for herself? If Thorburn were to marry into the Miranor family, our territory's security would be guaranteed."

"Obviously, the Emperor wouldn't allow their union. Unless, of course, Marshal Thorburn gave up all his military power... But that's not even the most important part. Only after hearing your story today did I remember another crucial piece of information."

Josephine paused, organising her thoughts.

"The basis of the rumour is that the Marshal once

admitted in private to having a daughter. He claimed the mother was a deceased commoner, so the girl was sent to an orphanage. He used this excuse to refuse arranged marriages with noble families. People speculated that the girl's age matched yours—hence the belief that you are the secret child of Lady Evelina and the Marshal."

"Wait, you mentioned an orphanage?!"

Valeria latched onto the key detail in the revelation.

"Perhaps the very orphanage you mentioned," Josephine suggested.

"Nina?! It's her?!" Valeria covered her mouth, lowering her voice.

"Who else could it be? From what you've said, she's an exceptional warrior, likely inheriting her father's combat skills—but being abandoned as a child, she might have chosen to join the Troglodyte resistance."

"And Geoffrey..." Valeria's concern shifted back to him.

"Maybe the Marshal secretly sent Geoffrey to assist Nina. It all makes sense now. But this could also become evidence against the Marshal—the Emperor has long been dissatisfied with him and is looking for an opportunity to weaken his power."

"Will they arrest Geoffrey for interrogation?"

The thought made Valeria's hands tremble; she feared that the kind-hearted Geoffrey might be sacrificed as a pawn against the Marshal.

"He is the key to the entire secret, so he's undoubtedly in grave danger," Josephine emphasised.

They looked at each other, one with tears in her eyes, the other with reddened eyes, and both were silent.

Josephine was the first to break the silence, speaking earnestly.

"Valeria, you are my only friend. I'm just an ordinary merchant's daughter; Lady Evelina and others don't care about my opinions. Although Celisara is a free and unrestrained place, it's not my home—I stayed on that unfamiliar star because you treated me as a friend. I understand the obsession of finding the one true meaning in your life. I can understand your feelings now—you've found the essence of life, and nothing else seems to matter. But can you, like me, abandon everything from your past and face danger together for that person?"

"I... I am willing."

Valeria's eyes sparkled.

Josephine's eyes lit up with excitement.

Then Valeria's gaze dimmed again.

She murmured, "But I don't want to put my mother in a difficult position... More importantly, she is our guardian, and yours as well. If she is harmed in this, all of Celisara might suffer. I don't want... our beautiful homeland to become like the surface of Zafirah I saw today."

Josephine nodded, understanding the implication.

Valeria knew she had to arm herself with reason and not let sudden love cloud her judgement—this was not just for her mother, for the Miranor family, or for Celisara, but also for Geoffrey's safety.

If she acted foolishly at the ball tomorrow, the

consequences could affect everyone she loved, including Geoffrey.

"Maybe they'll introduce you to some noble scions tomorrow, or they might announce an unfortunate marriage..."

Josephine showed a pained expression.

"Remember, endure, observe, cooperate, and then..."

"Strike first!"

"Catch them off guard!"

It was a tactic they learned in their flight lessons, taught by Lady Evelina.

"Tomorrow, at the ball, I'll try to greet the Marshal and find out the current situation in the Imperial Capital. Of course, I'll seek my mother's advice first..."

Valeria planned her "debut performance" for tomorrow.

"As for me... I'm not qualified to attend the ball, but I can help retrieve your aircraft and maybe meet the Marshal's illegitimate daughter."

Josephine looked at Valeria's profile lying next to her.

"We'll uncover the truth together and then make our plans."

Regarding Valeria's concerns about the Archons, Josephine offered her perspective.

"It seems to force Geoffrey to choose a side but doesn't want to kill him or you, the intruder... if it can be used..."

"That's too dangerous!"

"It's worth a try. But don't worry, I'm going

mainly to gather more information..."

"By the way, take this."

Valeria removed the medallion Geoffrey had given her from her necklace. Although she felt a pang of reluctance, she knew it was more important for Josephine to have it for her mission.

"Remember to return it to me... I'll be waiting for you, always waiting for your return. You must come back, whole."

"Of course, who else is Celisara's best mechanic?" Josephine said with a smile.

She was also Valeria's best friend.

The next evening, a welcome ball for the Miranor family was to be held at the Imperial Palace.

The day before, Markgräfin Evelina had already met with His Majesty the Emperor in her capacity as the Commander of the Border Military District.

As a result, she had hardly any time to inquire about her beloved daughter's whereabouts.

In the afternoon, a dressed-up Valeria arrived at her mother's resting room.

"Let me see the most beautiful sapphire of Celisara," Lady Evelina said with a smile.

She was not a woman who easily showed her emotions.

With deep cunning, she only revealed her true feelings in front of her daughter. When the door was open, she was the stern, decisive woman of power; when it was closed, she was a somewhat strict but affectionate mother.

Valeria gladly submitted to her mother's

inspection.

She mentally rehearsed the lines she and Josephine had practised yesterday, ready to "consult" her mother about the social nuances and people of the Imperial Capital.

"Mother, before the ball, I wanted to understand a few matters of etiquette... and the people involved."

The Markgräfin smiled knowingly.

"You want to ask me about my relationship with the Marshal, don't you?"

Valeria was too shocked to speak—she knew her beloved mother was an unconventional strategist, but she had not expected their first heart-to-heart conversation in her adulthood to begin with such a sensitive topic.

"Oh! Mother!"

Valeria could only express her surprise and implicit agreement through her tone.

Evelina continued, "I have always strived to be an enlightened parent, giving you the greatest freedom. Some things I kept from you for your own good—but now, since you must face the complexities of the Imperial Capital, I, as your mother and the head of our family, must tell you certain things."

"I'm listening."

Valeria grew serious, taking a deep breath. She was pleased that her mother finally saw her as more than just a child.

"When I was young, I did have a romance with the Marshal."

Evelina's lips curled into a slight, mysterious smile as she watched her daughter's reaction.

Valeria's mind raced through various speculations, her expression changing several times.

She held her breath, waiting for further explanation.

"Your biological father is not him—forgive me, but I'm not ready to reveal that person's name yet," Evelina said.

"It's alright, Mother. You can tell me whenever you're ready. It's your personal freedom."

"However, I learned from the Marshal yesterday that His Majesty plans to have you marry a Marshal."

Valeria's mind exploded with a buzzing noise, struggling to process the information.

"You also noticed I said 'a Marshal'—it doesn't necessarily mean the honourable Thorburn. The Emperor doesn't want us to marry into other families with fiefs, and he wants to take you from me, keeping you here as a hostage."

"I don't want that."

"Exactly, my dear daughter. A woman must learn to say 'no.'"

"What should I do? What will you do?"

Valeria eagerly sought her mother's guidance.

"You and I are different, Valeria. You may not achieve what I have done—and you don't have to be alone like me. You have your own choices, don't you?"

Evelina's gaze seemed to pierce through Valeria, but she didn't press the matter further.

Instead, she comforted her daughter, saying, "Tonight's ball is just for show. Just play your role well. If anything happens, I will help you. After all, I am your mother. But remember, all my choices are for the future of Celisara."

"I understand."

At that moment, Valeria couldn't fully grasp her mother's deeper intentions, but she deeply agreed with her mother's sentiment: Celisara was the most important.

Had it not been for Geoffrey showing her the dark side of Zafirah, Valeria might not have so clearly realised how many priceless treasures she already possessed.

She wanted Geoffrey to be happy too, though she knew it would be a long and arduous journey, not something that could be achieved overnight or through a small act of rebellion.

The key question—as her mother had asked—was: what was his answer?

Does he like me too? What is he struggling with internally? What does he want to achieve in this tumultuous Imperial Capital?

Valeria wanted to know everything about him.

Seeing the thoughtful look on her daughter's face, Evelina made another unexpected "attack."

"I heard that the one who brought you back yesterday was an honourable Imperial soldier."

Valeria was stunned, her face turning red.

She tried her best to hide the embarrassment of her secret being uncovered, but it was useless.

Her nervous demeanour had completely betrayed her.

"Yes..."

She took a deep breath and began recounting yesterday's dangerous yet fortunate adventure—she even forgot her original intent to conceal the crash of her flyer.

Evelina's expression turned serious as she listened to her daughter's story.

"Valeria, you trust people too easily. If not for Geoffrey, you might not be here today; your mother would have lost her most beloved daughter; your friends would have lost their best companion."

Valeria bowed her head in acknowledgment.

"What's even more frightening is that you let your friend handle this matter secretly—she, too, is in danger."

"Josephine... Oh, no!"

Valeria suddenly realised this point.

Her choice was based on trusting Geoffrey's influence among those people, but what if they had other plans?

Just as Valeria began to anxiously clutch her skirt hem, ready to leave, Evelina cradled her daughter's hand, resuming her calm demeanour.

"But fortunately, your mother also has many friends in the Imperial Capital. They will help us secretly."

Valeria looked at her mother with gratitude, surprise, and happiness.

People often said that Lady Evelina was a remarkable figure—not only valiant and strategic on the battlefield but also the most admired flower in the court.

Valeria had previously thought these were mere compliments, but now she felt a sense of safety and pride.

Seeing her daughter's emotions settle, Evelina continued her lesson in political philosophy.

"Listen, do not underestimate these balls. They are not merely grand spectacles. You must use your charm to conquer them, just as you would with firepower. In this arena, it's crucial to hide your emotions and true intentions. If they think you're an unsophisticated country girl, then play that role. But observe their every move carefully, listen to every idle word, as the most powerful strategies may start from a casual conversation over a lady's tea. You can win the friendship of an entire star system or gain rare mineral resources without spilling a drop of blood. Use these non-violent weapons to protect your people, family, and friends."

"And," Evelina cleared her throat, "if you have someone you like, do not be afraid to love them. But be cautious, as this could bring trouble or even disaster to both you and the other person. Consider the consequences and how to manage them. So, regardless of which lucky person the Emperor announces as your fiancé, do not act on impulse or sentiment. When the time comes, according to your wishes, I will help you achieve the desired outcome."

Valeria fully understood her mother's teachings and nodded firmly.

With that, their pre-ball conversation ended.

Evelina offered a few comforting words to ease Valeria's nerves before sending her daughter off on a new journey.

CHAPTER 3

The Gravity

The corridor leading to the ballroom was lined with many elegantly dressed aristocrats.

Valeria, surrounded by her striking companions of the same age, felt uneasy.

Josephine hadn't returned yet.

Although her attendants were not permitted inside the ballroom and could only accompany her to the entrance, Valeria now realised that Josephine was more than just a friend.

Valeria loved flight training but knew nothing about these prominent society people.

While her mother's teachings had been helpful, at this moment, she needed a meticulous attendant to remind her of every detail.

In Celisara, one's background was less important.

Among her attendants were several commoners, including Josephine.

They might be knowledgeable and highly skilled

in combat, but their understanding of court affairs was no better than Valeria's own.

How did Josephine know so many secrets?

She must have, as her mother suggested, carefully observed everyone's actions and listened intently to their casual conversations.

Josephine had always been an unassuming girl who spent most of her time listening to others.

But being quiet didn't mean she was incapable, which was a mistake many made by underestimating Josephine and treating her as just Valeria's little sidekick.

As Valeria was trying to handle the seemingly endless line of nobles greeting her and attempting to remember their families and names, she noticed a dark figure standing quietly in the corner.

She recognised him immediately—it was Geoffrey!

This Imperial soldier was not in his combat gear today. He wore a standard uniform, and his hair was neatly combed, looking much less casual than usual.

Geoffrey glanced her way occasionally, but dared not look directly at her.

Valeria's heart pounded.

She was excited and happy but also afraid of losing composure in front of others and exposing Geoffrey's presence and her connection to him to those who might harbour ill intentions toward her mother.

However, she couldn't control her gaze, which cut through the crowd and rested firmly on Geoffrey, even as a certain countess was speaking to her.

She felt as though she could sense his heartbeat—

how strange—like their hearts were resonating, creating the same eerie feeling she experienced in the cave yesterday.

Noticing Valeria looking at something, the crowd also turned to see what caught her attention.

Oh, no! Valeria regretted her action immediately.

Her mind raced, seeking a plausible explanation.

She quickly asked in a naïve tone, "Why are there so many soldiers here? Are all the Imperial balls also military meetings?"

The countess, clearly interpreting her question as the ignorance of a provincial noble, eagerly explained, with a hint of condescension.

"His Majesty the Emperor has always valued the military. It's not uncommon for many high-ranking officers to attend these balls. However, the ones you see here..."

"They're just my little guards," a voice interjected, "protecting all you lovely ladies. But close protection can only be entrusted to experienced old hands like me."

This voice was deep and magnetic, solemn yet humorous.

Its presence commanded silence from everyone, as if the speaker were the Emperor himself.

Hugh Thorburn had arrived.

He was the centre of the vortex, another key figure in today's ball—perhaps even more influential than Valeria in the eyes of the Empire.

Evelina had hinted to Valeria that Marshal Thorburn, despite his many military achievements, remained single, which displeased the minor nobles trying to curry favour with him, as well as the Emperor.

The Emperor's ambiguous suggestion of marrying Valeria to someone, without specifying whom, was a means to trouble Thorburn and keep Evelina in check —surely the Emperor had heard rumours about their relationship.

Politically, the Emperor would never want a powerful noble stationed at the frontier to marry a Marshal.

Militarily, Thorburn's achievements and popularity meant he always had a large group of followers wherever he went, and he could train formidable armies.

This dubious marriage arrangement seemed like a massive trap.

Valeria's thoughts raced, and she suddenly realised that the only outcomes for Thorburn might be death or perpetual imprisonment, as nothing else would ease the Emperor's fears.

Being in Thorburn's presence made Valeria acutely aware of these dangers.

These terrifying thoughts, once they appeared, grew uncontrollably.

Filled with curiosity, unease, and fear, she slowly turned her head and found a tall, well-proportioned, middle-aged man standing behind her.

He wore a neatly pressed military uniform adorned with many medals, his slightly curly black hair tousled.

His delicate features made him appear more like a god of beauty than a god of war.

Thorburn himself seemed indifferent to the intense attention and reverence directed at him, casually greeting the nearest ladies.

The silence was broken, and the ladies politely responded to his greetings.

Only Valeria noticed that Geoffrey, standing in the corner, seemed to transform—no longer leaning against the wall with his arms crossed.

He stood upright and gave a subtle, almost unnoticed military salute while his fellow guards remained motionless.

Strange... Valeria noted this odd reaction and looked toward Thorburn, lifting her skirt in a proper noble manner, and softly greeted, "Good day, esteemed Marshal."

"Oh, this must be the most beautiful sapphire of Celisara," the Marshal responded with a smile.

"You are almost as beautiful as your mother was in her youth."

"You flatter me."

After a brief exchange of pleasantries, Thorburn escorted Valeria into the ballroom.

However, rather than feeling courted by an admirer, Valeria felt their conversation resembled that of a teacher and student, or a parent and child.

For a moment, Valeria wished Thorburn were her biological father, or that her mother could marry this charming man and make him her stepfather—it wouldn't matter at all...

Such a Thorburn was both lovable and intimidating. He was equally loved and hated.

Taking a deep breath, Valeria stepped through the

doors of the ballroom—out of the corner of her eye. She saw Geoffrey watching her with a complex expression.

She felt as though she could sense his emotions, which seemed like jealousy—but not the kind born of romantic feelings.

Geoffrey must admire the Marshal, she thought, but he was only an ordinary soldier under Thorburn's command.

After the ball, she resolved to talk to Geoffrey alone.

On one hand, she wanted to express her feelings and affection; on the other, she hoped to learn more about the Marshal and Nina from Geoffrey.

Thus, the ball begun with the announcement that His Majesty the Emperor would be absent.

The Emperor was unwell and gifted each guest a bottle of aged royal Zafirah liquor, named "Emperor Toman"—a bottle valuable enough to purchase the property of a small star system.

Although Toman was an ancestor of the former Eldaric family, the usurper did not shy away from its past glory.

As for the imperial decree, it was likely to be read out near the end of the ball.

Valeria was restless.

She guessed the Emperor wanted to keep everyone in suspense and had sent people to secretly observe, to identify traitors or gather evidence against the Marshal.

Every move she made was the focus of everyone's

attention.

She felt like the core of a black hole, absorbing the gazes of those around her.

According to court etiquette, the guide and companion should dance the first dance together to show respect and gratitude.

Evelina did not accompany Valeria, and now Valeria believed it was her mother who had the Marshal fetch her.

Evelina later appeared with a young nobleman whom Valeria did not know—he must have been one of her friends in the Imperial Capital.

Following various formalities, they bowed to each other and then started to dance.

This was Valeria's debut, and she wanted to perform well.

But her nervousness made her movements stiff and unnatural.

The Marshal, of course, noticed this and kindly guided her, saying, "Imagine it's like two people balancing on a beam over water, spinning together."

Thorburn's words not only shifted Valeria's focus but also shocked her.

The Marshal knew about the cave incident?

Could Nina truly be his illegitimate daughter?!

Her intense curiosity made Valeria forget she was performing, her attention fully on Thorburn's gentle and loving face.

He didn't seem like a soldier, more like... like Geoffrey.

"What else do you know?" she couldn't help but ask, keeping the question vague.

"I know your little secret in that cave... yes, my daughter told me," Thorburn said with no pretence.

"Your daughter?"

Valeria feigned ignorance.

"Oh, yes. Some say it's a scandal meant to ruin my reputation, while others claim it's a rumour I spread to stay single—but they're all wrong. I've always wanted a daughter, a lovely daughter like you. Sometimes I envy Evelina. After we parted ways, I had my girl with my partner. But I can't publicly acknowledge that child."

Nina didn't seem lovely.

Valeria recalled their unpleasant first encounter—Nina was practically synonymous with fierceness and cunning, and the strange and terrifying Archons possessed her.

But hearing it from the Marshal, Nina seemed pitiful.

Valeria's feelings became complicated.

On one hand, there was Nina's background and current situation.

On the other, the Emperor might target the kind and humorous Thorburn, with Valeria herself possibly being used as a pawn against him.

And if Nina's lineage were revealed, it could be used against the Marshal.

Serving a ruler was indeed like accompanying a tiger.

This made Valeria recall the strange behaviour of the Imperial soldiers at the entrance.

She thought, apart from Geoffrey, the other soldiers didn't seem to respect or like Thorburn very much.

Perhaps the Emperor's plans were more extensive, and maybe Geoffrey had something important to convey to her but couldn't say outright.

Considering that Geoffrey had once assisted Thorburn in the cave, Valeria believed he must be one of Thorburn's trusted aides.

Unable to contain her curiosity, she asked, "So, did you send Geoffrey to help her?"

"Geoffrey? Help her?"

Thorburn responded with some confusion.

Thorburn's reaction puzzled Valeria as well—hadn't he sent someone to help his own daughter? Wasn't that the natural thing to do?

Just as Valeria worried she might have said something wrong to upset the Marshal, an imperial eunuch entered the room with a decree.

Because of concerns about the Archons, the eunuchs serving the Emperor were pure-blooded humans, unaware of their parents or families.

They were selected from the moment of fertilisation and castrated at an appropriate age to maintain purity, with special devices implanted in their brains to ensure loyalty.

Their purpose was to serve the Empire, a practice unchanged through several dynasties.

The eunuch read aloud, "His Majesty the Emperor gives the most sacred marriage contract upon the Imperial Marshal, and Lady Valeria of the Miranor family."

Everyone's eyes turned to the pair who had just finished their dance.

Valeria, who had been worried about this marriage contract, now felt a sense of relief.

Thorburn didn't seem like a bad person, and her mother must have had an agreement with the Marshal to resolve this issue.

She glanced at the Marshal, but from his expression, she saw an unfamiliar worry and gravity.

The calm smile disappeared from Thorburn's face.

The decree continued, "Effective immediately, Hugh Thorburn will step down as Imperial Marshal. Corin of Nebula Cloude will assume all his powers and duties."

Corin stepped forward.

He had dark skin, long silver hair, and a handsome face, exuding confidence and arrogance.

Nebula Cloude was a relatively remote and independent region within the galaxy.

It was named because a group of stars had collapsed and exploded during a war, enclosing the habitable area and making entry and exit difficult.

The descendants of the survivors there lived by navigating and fighting in space, becoming ferocious.

Interestingly, the settlers and their descendants had adapted to the peculiar cosmic radiation and could change their skin colour at will.

Corin evidently believed his current appearance suited the role of the future Marshal.

This meant Valeria's fiancé was Corin, the man who had accompanied Evelina earlier.

Valeria was thrown into chaos.

She almost fainted—the feeling of almost falling in

the cave swept over her again, but this time it was not fear but anger.

She glanced at Corin.

Corin, not much older than Valeria, had notable military achievements but lacked political acumen.

He clumsily waved and smiled at Valeria.

Valeria didn't think Corin was evil, but had no liking for him, so she ignored his greeting.

Then she looked at her mother.

Evelina's gaze seemed to say, "You can't trust anyone; I warned you."

She tried to peer through the servant's entrance, hoping to glimpse Geoffrey, but he was nowhere to be found.

Finally, she looked at Thorburn.

The Marshal's eyes showed some relief, but no resentment—yet she also saw a trace of sorrow and regret in his gaze.

Thorburn had been forcibly removed from the stage of the Imperial Capital.

Valeria was surprised that the Marshal neither defended himself nor resisted.

The handover ceremony ended briefly and peacefully.

Having shed his honour-laden uniform and now dressed in just a shirt and jacket, former Marshal Thorburn seemed to complain to Evelina before leaving, his words full of meaning.

"Quite unexpected... I thought you'd agree if our children fell in love."

"Sorry, I have other plans. That child... I can't let

them be together because he is..."

"Just because he's my child?"

"Yes."

After Evelina's reply, Thorburn left in dismay.

Their words stirred ripples in Valeria's heart—wait, I fell in love with the Marshal's child?! Me and Nina?!

No, that's not right!

It's... Geoffrey?!

Geoffrey is the Marshal's "daughter"?!

Valeria ran out.

She wasn't looking for Thorburn, but for Geoffrey.

However, when she reached the door, she couldn't find the one who made her heart race.

Disregarding etiquette, she grabbed a soldier who was gloating over the old Marshal's downfall and asked, "Geoffrey? Do you know him? Where is he?"

The soldier, seeing it was Lady Valeria asking, dared not ignore her.

He stammered, "He... he followed old Thorburn somewhere, I don't know where."

The ball was interrupted, and the scene became chaotic.

Other guests also poured out, and Valeria was soon lost in the crowd.

She paid no attention to the surrounding commotion, only thinking about how to find that father and son—or rather, father and daughter.

Thinking back now, Geoffrey did resemble Thorburn.

Perhaps part of the attraction she felt towards Thorburn stemmed from her feelings for Geoffrey.

She didn't even care if Geoffrey was a girl. She just wanted to know if Geoffrey felt the same way — whether Geoffrey was struggling with her identity and gender, hence not daring to speak out.

Or was it all just her own dreaming?

While Valeria was lost in thought and feeling a vague pain in her heart, she heard her mother calling.

"Valeria, we're leaving the Imperial Capital. Corin will give us a clear path; he promised we could return to our home planet. But we must leave quickly."

At some point, Evelina had already changed into combat gear, and she tossed a set to Valeria as well.

But Valeria stood there, stunned.

"Is this the deal you made with your friend?" she asked, gripping the combat suit tightly.

"Yes, but it's not the complete story. I have little time to explain. Chaos is about to erupt in the Imperial Capital. The old fool underestimated Thorburn's influence."

Valeria didn't need any further explanation from her mother.

She understood very well that all of her mother's decisions were for Celisara and Miranor.

So, no more words were necessary.

Suddenly, Valeria felt clearer.

"What about Josephine?"

"She has already contacted the mothership. She will set off directly and meet us in orbit."

Finally, hearing some good news, Valeria silently prayed for Josephine.

Before leaving, Valeria desperately wanted to see Geoffrey again.

But her mother's resolute gaze told her that everything was over.

It was just a summer love dream, and now it was time to wake up.

Valeria felt reluctant, but she also respected and admired her mother, just as Geoffrey did his father.

So, with a heavy and sorrowful heart, Valeria returned to the geostationary orbit.

The journey was not peaceful.

As her mother had said, Thorburn's influence seemed to exceed the Emperor's expectations—for better or worse.

The Troglodyte rebels seemed to stir, making Josephine's return more perilous.

And in orbit, as Valeria and her mother travelled in the shuttle, they saw unidentified objects suddenly appearing.

These warships, leaping from who knows where, were menacing, with some dispatching landing crafts and others clearing Imperial ships in orbit.

Corin had sent several small warships to escort the guests from Miranor and his fiancée, but they were all sacrificed.

Eventually, Evelina and Valeria safely reached the mothership, Neowise.

As soon as Evelina returned to the ship, she began organising the evacuation.

They received a signal from Josephine during the manoeuvre, but the recently repaired small flyer's thrust was insufficient for a quick return, so Neowise had to circle and wait for the right moment.

Compared to Geoffrey, Valeria was now more

worried about Josephine's safety.

She believed Thorburn would protect his child.

But Josephine?

In this world, who else remembered her besides Valeria?

Valeria had indeed taken her mother's words to heart.

If she couldn't protect her best friend, how could she one day inherit Miranor?

"I want to rescue Josephine. Mother, please allow me," Valeria said firmly.

Evelina looked at her daughter with gratification and nodded.

"I have a coming-of-age gift for you."

In the hangar of Neowise, a silver-white combat airship was pushed out from behind a curtain.

Its surface was sleek, displaying a top level of technology—it resembled Celisara's eternal ice crystals, shimmering but revealing nothing of its internal structure from any angle.

"This is Glacia. It has stealth capabilities and is exceptional in space combat. Valeria, it is now yours."

Piloting the Glacia, Valeria appeared on the battlefield.

Following her mother's instructions, she did not engage in the chaotic battle but focused on searching for Josephine.

The small spacecraft, one of her coming-of-age gifts, had no combat capabilities and lacked both a number and a name, making it appear quite ordinary.

Despite this, Valeria felt apologetic towards the vessel, now battered from her own recklessness.

Fortunately, her search was fruitful.

Soon, she spotted a small craft wobbling upwards, evading space debris—a speck invisible to the naked eye but already displayed on Glacia's screen.

"Excellent!"

Valeria cried with joy.

The sorrow of missing Geoffrey was momentarily eased.

"Josephine! Hurry!" she called through the communicator.

"Valeria, look who's here!"

Josephine responded, bringing up the cockpit visuals.

"Is it Geoffrey?"

Hope rekindled in Valeria's heart, but she saw an unexpected figure on the screen.

It was Nina.

But Nina's response was even more surprising.

"It's me. I am Geoffrey."

"What is happening?"

Valeria's emotions, a mix of sorrow and joy, overflowed into tears.

It seemed Josephine was grumbling on the other side.

"Just spit it out already!"

Valeria waited for the answer.

Geoffrey responded.

It was a silent answer.

The gravity that had seemed like a harbinger of doom no longer terrified her.

Suddenly, Valeria's vision became broad and

clear, allowing her to see everything at the centre of the gravitational field—something was pulsating there.

Something was invading her body, as if trying to connect with her nerves.

Then she saw the twinkling of stars, and the planet Zafirah below her warped and distorted.

No sound, no words, only the rhythm of her heartbeat echoed like ripples in a gravity field, forming a bond with another resonating presence.

Valeria's intuition told her it was Geoffrey—though "she" was now in Nina's body, "she" was the one Valeria had always known and loved.

A strange, twisted wave intertwined the two of them, their emotions resonating across the cosmos like ripples.

"So that's it..." Valeria choked out.

Geoffrey must be an Archon, and perhaps Thorburn was too.

It had nothing to do with gender.

Geoffrey wasn't even human—a being perceived as the most sinister high-dimensional entity by human society.

But that did not hinder Valeria's love—she knew it had nothing to do with these external matters.

From the moment Geoffrey's gravity captured her, she had fallen into a galaxy named love.

She also understood that Geoffrey had just expressed mutual affection.

On this summer night, under the starry sky, their spirits were eternally intertwined.

This was a realm beyond human consciousness,

so Valeria was still perceiving everything with human cognition.

Through Geoffrey's guidance, she saw everything happening on the entire planet and the impending disaster.

The unknown ship's attack was directed at them.

Although the actions appeared slow from a higher-dimensional perspective, she couldn't perform any countermeasures.

She could now see every organ, cell, and organelle in her body, but she couldn't use her hands to manoeuvre the combat spacecraft because she had lost control of her physical body.

After all, she was human and lacked certain abilities.

"No—"

Her consciousness wailed, falling from the stars back to the material world.

Geoffrey and Josephine's spacecraft had no attack capabilities, and Valeria, having just returned to her body, still could not control herself.

The attack in the actual dimension was incredibly swift; it seemed bombs would hit the two small ships in mere moments.

A scream echoed from the other end of the communication.

Am I going to die? Am I going to die here with Geoffrey?

As Valeria's thoughts spiralled, she suddenly noticed the attack being distorted by something invisible, deflecting it harmlessly—both for Geoffrey and Josephine, as well.

Saved!

By whom?

"Youngsters are always so hasty," came "Nina's," voice over the communicator.

But Valeria recognised that tone—sometimes terrifyingly solemn, sometimes kindly humorous.

"Phantom. Or rather, Mr Thorburn."

"Sorry, the situation is urgent. I could only send Geoffrey back to the surface. Their target should be me, and the distortion just now might have alerted them further."

Then Thorburn spoke to Josephine, who was too shocked to speak.

"Young lady, open the hatch."

"Here?!"

"Not only enemies are coming, but also my allies."

Indeed, just as Thorburn opened the cockpit and flew out, a small, ragged-looking yet fast-moving ship rushed over.

It appeared to be a re-built civilian ship, thus avoiding deliberate attacks.

"Thanks for the combat suit," Thorburn whispered to Valeria.

"Its airtightness is excellent. Also, give my regards to your mother."

Josephine's spacecraft finally reached a safe altitude.

The two best friends, though still shaken, were extremely grateful.

They didn't need to communicate through minds or words; a simple instant message confirming their safety was enough, like two birds returning to the nest in their mother's embrace.

"This is a letter from Geoffrey to you, and here's the pendant she returned."

Josephine's first words upon seeing Valeria made her cry with joy.

"She said she wasn't sure if there would be time to talk or if you two could meet again, so she wrote down what she wanted to say and gave it to me to pass to you. There should be contact details—though I reckon they'll be busy for a while."

Indeed, Zafirah had turned into a chaotic battlefield as her mother had foreseen.

But after witnessing Thorburn's abilities, Valeria believed Geoffrey would not be in mortal danger.

She knew what the letter said, with no need to read it.

She knew Geoffrey loved her, just as she loved Geoffrey.

When two people are connected in spirit, even in the far reaches of the universe, their hearts beat as one.

Geoffrey was not lost amidst the chaos of the court.

When he saw Thorburn stepping out, he wanted to follow, but the crowd blocked his way, preventing him from getting close immediately.

However, as a soldier, Geoffrey's determination made it possible for him to follow through.

Thorburn did not evade anyone; he simply left the detestable court as quickly as possible—as if staying a second longer would taint him with its stench.

Thus, when Thorburn exited the palace and slipped into a nearby military building, Geoffrey was already on his trail.

"Please tell me the truth, Lord Thorburn," Geoffrey demanded, suppressing his confusion and anger, standing in front of Thorburn.

For a long time, he had regarded Thorburn as his faith.

Thorburn, born a commoner, had distinguished himself in battle and never forgot the suffering of the commoners and cave dwellers, often helping them in secret.

This quality, especially, earned Geoffrey's admiration.

He aspired to be like Thorburn.

Thorburn had always been kind in teaching him combat skills, even showing a bit of favouritism towards Geoffrey among the many subordinates, which sparked jealousy and rumours.

Perhaps what Geoffrey didn't know was that Thorburn had always shown a bit of favouritism towards talented students.

Evelina had once been one of his students.

But Geoffrey's intuition told him that Thorburn's attention towards him carried a bit more weight.

Later, Thorburn gave him private lessons—while this made Geoffrey feel honoured, it also made him suspect he might be the rumoured illegitimate child.

Many people speculated about this or thought Geoffrey was Thorburn's bustard son and future successor.

It was the day after he started receiving private

lessons from Thorburn that he first witnessed the so-called "Phantom" in the cave.

He didn't make the connection.

Subsequently, Nina often became possessed by the Phantom, relaying some obscure messages to Geoffrey.

But at the time, he thought they were hallucinations.

Until today's ball.

Geoffrey, listening to the other soldiers and servants gossiping about the situation inside, erupted with uncontrollable emotions upon learning about the engagement.

He was terrified of losing Valeria—the adorable alien princess who had stolen his heart at first sight.

But he was even more shocked at the hasty and careless transition of the marshal's position.

Geoffrey was still unknown and young, clearly unfit for the marshal's duties.

But having an outsider from another realm take power, along with Thorburn seeming to accept this reality—Geoffrey couldn't accept such an outcome.

He knew Thorburn's prowess, both in combat and strategy.

Therefore, he was discontent with the former marshal's easy surrender.

He also wanted to win back Valeria.

Perhaps for the first time in his life, he had a personal desire—beyond protecting the capital's commoners and maintaining peace in the universe.

Thorburn was a powerful man, but he had given up so easily—what about Geoffrey?

As a weak, ordinary soldier of the Empire, how could he resist imperial power?

So, he had to confront Thorburn face-to-face and get the answers he needed.

However, the former marshal's first unexpected attack pierced through Geoffrey's defences.

"Do you still want to see her?"

"Nina? Is she your child?"

"No, I mean your beloved. My child. You are all my children."

Geoffrey's head buzzed.

It seemed he had subconsciously grasped a more complex answer, but he couldn't describe it.

"Time is running out. Do you still want to see her?"

"Yes."

Geoffrey did not hide or hesitate.

"Then there's still a chance, as long as she hasn't left the planet's gravitational field."

"But the spaceport is already under control. Even if we seize a shuttle or a fighter, we won't have a chance..."

"Of course, we're not using such foolish human methods," Thorburn laughed.

Geoffrey's mind buzzed again.

Thorburn continued, "My child, you can do it. If you want to, you can catch up to her."

These words acted like a switch, suddenly illuminating Geoffrey's mind.

Finally, Geoffrey understood what Thorburn was describing.

He was being pulled by a mysterious force that

didn't belong to him or the world, propelling him skyward.

He now had only one thought in his mind: to see Valeria, to tell her he loved her, and to never be separated.

This thought broadened his mind and lifted him higher and higher.

Geoffrey seemed to sense a presence with a wavelength very similar to his own.

It was Nina.

Her body was on the small spacecraft that Valeria had unfortunately left behind.

But what about Nina's spirit?

Geoffrey seemed to detect another channel flickering. He immediately knew that was Nina, but she was going somewhere else and would be back shortly.

Nina told Geoffrey he could use her body.

Geoffrey did not hesitate and descended.

At the moment he plugged in the body, Geoffrey seemed to remember something—a childhood memory that had long been blurred.

It was from the early life Nina had lived.

Back then, "she" was not called Nina, but had another name. She had a stern father but no mother.

However, this moment of emotion did not make her forget what she wanted to do.

She asked the brave female pilot for a portable memory device that humans could read, so she could write down her love and longing for Valeria and exchange their contact information.

The spacecraft's communication was turned on,

and Geoffrey heard Valeria's voice.

At that moment, she couldn't control herself.

She wanted not only to pass the memory device to Valeria but also to deeply connect with her consciousness.

Geoffrey flew towards Valeria, her core pulsating and heading towards Valeria's core.

To the current Geoffrey, Valeria's core shone so brightly.

The rhythm and beat were perfect, a beauty that human senses could not fathom.

Their wavelengths overlapped, intertwining into a sonata.

I like you.

I love you.

Valeria, my tuner.

Words From The Author

After deciding to expand this story into a full-length novel, I rewrote the latter half of this novella to serve as a prequel to *Starlight Sonata*. Yes, it will be part of a trilogy about Lady Evelina's love story—though I must warn you, it will be a complex tale filled with court intrigue, power struggles, and interstellar wars, with our marvellous Lady Evelina playing a crucial role.

Readers who finish this prequel will undoubtedly sense my affection for this lady—she is beautiful and strong, full of cunning yet very idealistic. Of course, her daughter is also a charming character, though still immature.

Female characters will hold significant roles in the novel—alongside the wondrous aliens, or rather, beings I find hard to describe as merely "people." I prefer to call them space faeries.

Geoffrey's awakening is another fascinating aspect, though the prequel only covers the general outline. In the main story, Geoffrey seems destined to experience much more.

I have always harboured an ambition to write a science fiction space opera that is not so dark—yet it is not about a heroic epic where someone saves the entire universe, but an exploration of higher levels of human mind and consciousness. (Yes, it's the opposite of *Dune*!)

That might require some romance to explain.

Because of the multitude of characters, the main trilogy will present them through their respective POVs. I was inspired by *A Song of Ice and Fire* and have recently been watching *House of the Dragon*—but I've transported them to a futuristic space setting filled with light and hope.

And then there's my favourite French writer's court historical novels—perhaps some of you can guess the inspiration for Geoffrey and Valeria: if you've read the third part of that famous *Three Musketeers* trilogy, you'll know exactly what I'm talking about!

If you are interested, please subscribe to my mailing list to stay updated on my upcoming works. I also invite ARC readers to join. Please click here to learn more.

Jacqueline Westwoods

About the Author

Jacqueline Westwood is the pen name for romantic novels by a science fiction writer.

In Jacqueline's stories, the universe is bright, the human heart is dark, and only love can conquer all. She enjoys intricate character relationships—including romances—but believes that fate ultimately decides everything.

As an enthusiast of science fiction and fantasy, Jacqueline aims to create more female and queer characters within these genres. She is a supporter of multiculturalism and a part of it herself. She hopes people fall in love because of the attraction of their souls, not their bodies.

If you are interested, please subscribe to Jacqueline's mailing list to stay updated on her latest works.

Also, you may follow on Instagram:
@sffrauthorjackie

This is a work of fiction.

Names, characters, places, and incidents either are products of the author's imagination or are used fictitiously.

Any similarity to actual events or locales or persons, living or dead, is entirely coincidental.

BEATS OF LOVE

Copyright © 2024 by Jacqueline Westwoods

All rights reserved.

No part of this publication may be reproduced, distributed, or transmitted in any form or by any means, including photocopying, recording, or other electronic or mechanical methods, without the prior written permission of the publisher, except in the case of brief quotations embodied in critical reviews and certain other noncommercial uses permitted by copyright law.

Published by
HELIOPOLIS PRESS

Unit B, 12F, 28 Yee Wo Street
Causeway Bay, Hong Kong

www.heliopolis.press

Heliopolis Press® is a registered trademark of
Heliopolis Creative and Culture Limited

www.heliopolis-cc.com

The Hong Kong Public Library has cataloged the
<u>hardcover</u> edition as follows:

Name: Westwoods, Jacqueline. Author.
Title: Beats of Love / Jacqueline Westwoods.
Description: First edition. | Hong Kong: Heliopolis
Press, 2024.
Identifiers: ISBN 978-988-70531-1-8 (ebook)
Subjects: Science Fiction | Romance
Classification: F | Fiction

ISBN 978-988-70531-2-5 (Hardcover)

Our books may be purchased in bulk for promotional,
educational, or business use. Please contact your local
bookseller or the Heliopolis Press Sales Department by
email at sale@heliopolis.press

First Edition: August, 2024
First Hardcover Edition: August, 2024

Printed in Hong Kong

Milton Keynes UK
Ingram Content Group UK Ltd.
UKHW042021300724
446355UK00002B/19

9 789887 053125